For the shepherd and his lambs—
Flea, Sara, and James

Four Winds Press
Macmillan Publishing Company
866 Third Avenue, New York, NY 10022
First published 1990 in Great Britain by Walker Books, Ltd, London
First American edition 1990
Printed and bound in Italy

10   9   8   7   6   5   4   3   2   1

Library of Congress Cataloging-in-Publication Data
Lewis, Kim.
The shepherd boy.
Summary: James longs for the day he is old enough to
be a shepherd like his father, and when Christmas comes,
almost a year later, he receives a very special present.
[1. Shepherds—Fiction]   I. Title.
PZ7.L58723Sh   1990   [E]   89-23679
ISBN 0-02-758581-6

The Shepherd Boy

Kim Lewis

FOUR WINDS PRESS   NEW YORK

James's father was a shepherd. Every day he got up very early, took his crook and his collie, and went off to see his sheep.

James longed to be a shepherd too.

"You'll have to wait until you're a little older," his father said.

So every day James watched and waited.

James watched and waited all through spring. He watched as the new lambs were born, and saw them grow big and strong.

James watched and waited all through summer. He watched his father clip the sheep, and saw his mother pack the sacks of wool.

James watched and waited all through autumn. He watched his mother help to wean the lambs, and saw his father dip the sheep.

On market day, James
waited while the lambs
were sold and heard the
farmers talk of winter.

When snow fell, James watched his father feed the hungry sheep near the house, and saw him take hay on the tractor to the sheep on the hill.

Then James waited for his father to come home.

On Christmas Day, James and his father and mother opened their presents under the tree.

James found a crook and a cap and a brand-new dog whistle of his very own.

In a basket in the barn,
James found a collie puppy.
James's father read the card
on the puppy's neck.
It said: *My name is Jess.*
I belong to a shepherd boy
called James.

When spring came
again, James got up very
early. He took his crook
and his cap, and called
Jess with his whistle.

Then James and his
father went off to the
fields together.